This Little Tiger book belongs to:

_____

_____

_____

For Mom, Dad, and Meg
~ M. B.

LITTLE TIGER PRESS

1 The Coda Centre, 189 Munster Road, London SW6 6AW
www.littletiger.co.uk

First published in Great Britain 2005
by Little Tiger Press, London
This edition published 2013

Printed in China • LTP/1900/0723/0713

10 9 8 7 6 5 4 3 2

The Not So Abominable Snowman

Matt Buckingham

LITTLE TIGER PRESS

Have you ever heard of the Abominable Snowman?
There are lots of them, you know. They live high
in the mountains, in the deep, white snow.

They're covered in hair

and have huge feet,

long strong arms

and gnashing white teeth.

Bert was an abominable snowman. He liked
the snowy mountains, but he also liked to play
in the thick forests far below. There he'd run,
jump, climb, crawl, and chase butterflies.

One day Bert was chasing two butterflies when
they landed on a rock. Quietly he crept toward them.
But on the other side of the rock was a little BOY.
What a fright! He'd never seen such a sight!

Bert quickly dived into a bush to hide.
"AAAAWWWWWW!" Spiky thorns covered
him from head to toe!

The little boy walked over to Bert. "I'm sorry,"
he said. "I didn't mean to scare you. My name's
Tom. Who are you?"

"I'm Bert, an abominable snowman," said Bert.

"Oh! You don't look abominable to me," said Tom.

While Tom pulled the thorns from Bert's foot, he told Bert that he was worried about his father. "I'm waiting for him here while he climbs up the mountain, but he's been so long, something must be wrong."

"Let's look for him," said Bert and he lifted Tom onto his shoulders.

Dashing through the thick bamboo, they
met a giant panda.
  "Hello, panda," said Bert. "Have you
seen a grown man pass by?"

"He passed nearby, before climbing up high," the panda said, and he began to chew on some bamboo.

As Bert and Tom climbed higher, the thick forest turned
to grassy slopes. There they met a herd of cattle grazing.
   "Hello, yaks," said Bert. "Have you seen a grown
man pass by?"

"He walked this way, but didn't stay," said one
yak, and went back to munching the grass.

As the mountain grew steeper, the snow became
deeper. They saw a leopard slinking along.
"Hello, leopard," said Bert. "Have you seen
a grown man pass by?"

The leopard stopped and pointed higher up.
"I was roaming about when I heard a shout,"
she said, before going on her way.

They were nearly at the top of the mountain but there was still no sign of Tom's father. Tom was very worried.

"We could do with some help," said Bert, and he began to dance. THUMP! THUMP! THUMP! went his feet on the icy snow.

Suddenly, they heard a faint rumble that grew into
a deafening stampede. The ground began to shake,
as lots and lots of abominable snowmen appeared.

As soon as Bert had told his friends about Tom's father, the tallest snowmen clambered onto each other's shoulders to make a tower.

Bert climbed to the top. From there he could
see for miles. Far, far away he spotted some
tracks in the snow.

"I know where he is. Follow me!" said Bert,
and he jumped to the ground, picked Tom up
and raced off. They ran many many miles.

When they finally stopped, Bert pointed to
a hole in the snow. "Down there!" he said.

Then the snowmen made a long chain that stretched down into a crevasse.

At the bottom

of the crevasse

in a cold heap

was Tom's father.

"Hello," said Bert. "I'm Bert. I've come to help."

Bert carefully picked up Tom's father and gave a shout. The snowmen hauled everyone back to safety.

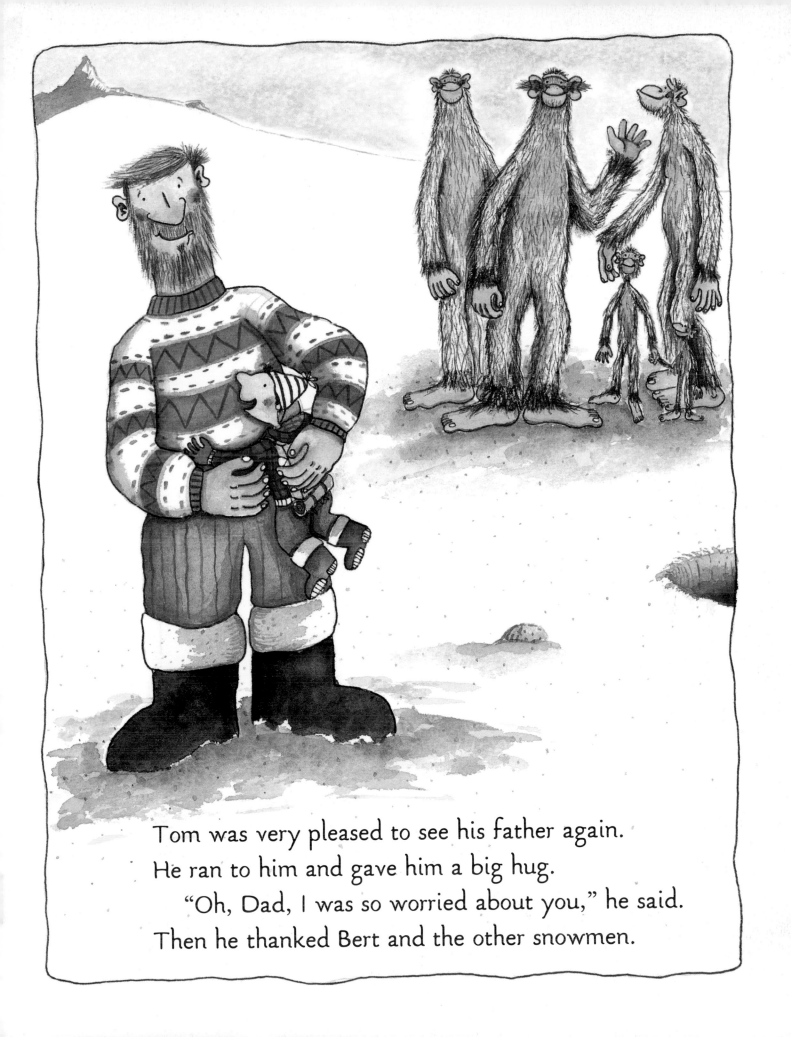

Tom was very pleased to see his father again.
He ran to him and gave him a big hug.
   "Oh, Dad, I was so worried about you," he said.
Then he thanked Bert and the other snowmen.

Bert sadly waved goodbye to his new friends.
As Tom and his father made their way down
the mountain, he saw Tom point to some
huge footprints in the snow.

"You know, Dad?" Tom said. "Bert's not so
abominable, is he? In fact, none of them are."